Animals are Sleeping

By Suzanne Slade

Illustrated by Gary R. Phillips

upside down,

down below,

below the ground.

curled on the snow,

perched in a tree,

warm on a rock,

floating free.

Shhh . . . shhh . . .
the animals are sleeping . . .

cat nap,

deep sleep,

quick wink,

without a peep.

Shhh . . . shhh . . .
the animals are sleeping

in the broad daylight,

In the still of night,

. . . the animals are sleeping.
Good night, sleep tight.

For Creative Minds

Animal Sorting Cards & Activities

Sleeping Animal Matching Activity: Guess which animal goes with each fun fact by matching it to the art. Answers are upside down on the bottom of each page. Copied cards can be sorted by animal class or what the animals eat.

Clownfish
Fish
eats pieces of dead fish and plankton
(carnivore)

Flamingo
Mammal
eats algae, insects, and small fish
(omnivore)

Sloth
Mammal
eats leaves, young plants, and fruit
(herbivore)

1. **Hanging upside down**, a_____sleeps 15 to 18 hours during the day. It holds tightly to a branch with its strong claws while sleeping soundly. Not even a loud rainforest thunderstorm will wake it. When the sun goes down, it finally moves from its sleeping position.

2. With perfect balance, a_____often **sleeps standing on one leg** facing into the wind. It folds the other leg neatly beneath its body and rests its head by tucking its beak under one wing.

3. This brightly colored_____lives in the warm waters of the Pacific Ocean. This tiny fish protects itself from enemies searching for a tasty meal by **hiding inside** an animal called a sea anemone. The long, flowing arms of the anemone will sting most sea creatures, but the poison in its arms does not hurt the fish. At night, the fish snuggles into its cozy sea anemone bed. The anemone's soft arms close around it, keeping it comfortable and safe until morning.

Answers: 1. sloth, 2. flamingo, 3. clownfish

Bee-eater
Bird
eats bees and insects
(carnivore)

Lizard
Reptile
most eat insects and
bug, some eat plants
(carnivore, some
omnivore)

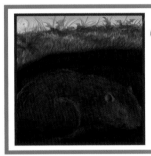

Groundhog
Mammal
eats mostly plants
and some insects
(omnivore)

Polar Bear
Mammal
eats seals and
other animals
(carnivore)

1. A_____is a cold-blooded animal. Its body does not make heat, so it must find heat to warm itself. **Stretching on a sunny rock** is the perfect place for a nap on a cool morning.

2. Exposed and dozing on the snow, a_____and her cubs stay surprisingly warm. These bears dig and then **snuggle into shallow pits** in the snow with their backs to the wind. Thick fur and a layer of fat keep them warm. A mother bear makes a soft pillow for her cubs.

3. The_____is famous for its sleeping habits. It hibernates, or sleeps, all winter long **curled in an underground burrow**. During hibernation its heartbeat and breathing slows down and its body temperature drops. There is a special day (February 2) in honor of this animal. Some people believe that if he sees his shadow when he comes out of hibernation, there will be six more weeks of winter.

4. A tiny_____likes to **sleep together with others at night**. Up to ten will line up on the same perch, arriving before dusk to claim their place in line. They all face the same direction and press their sides against each other before closing their eyes to sleep.

Answers: 1. lizard, 2. polar bear, 3. groundhog, 4. bee-eater

Giraffe
Mammal

eats leaves
(herbivore)

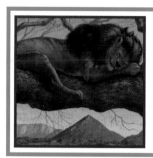

Lion
Mammal

eats other animals
(carnivore)

Harbor Seal
Mammal

eats fish and other
animals
(carnivore)

Koala
Mammal

eats plants
(herbivore)

1. Living high in eucalyptus trees, an Australian_____spends most of its life sleeping. It usually sleeps 18 to 20 hours each day. It **tucks into a fork of tree branches** to snooze.

2. A_____may **sleep on the beach or while floating in water**. It is lulled to sleep as it gently bobs up and down with only its head above water.

3. A_____sleeps about five minutes at a time, **standing up**. It sleeps about six times a day for a total of about 30 minutes.

4. **Curled on a limb** of a shade tree or stretched out on a rock, a_____takes many catnaps during the day. If it has a full stomach, it may sleep up to 20 hours a day.

Elephant
Mammal

eats leaves and plants
(herbivore)

Barn Owl
Bird

eats small animals
(carnivore)

Human
Mammal

eats plants and
animals
(omnivore)

Common Swift
Bird

eats bugs and insects
(carnivore)

1. A_____leaves its baby chicks for several days when it hunts for food. While the parents are gone, the young birds enter a deep sleep, called torpor, for up to ten days. Some adults **sleep while flying**, called "sleeping on the wing." At night, they fly above a pocket of warm air (about 3,000 to 6,000 feet above ground) and flap their wings about every four seconds as they sleep.

2. _____babies sleep about 16 hours a day. As they get older, they need less sleep. Children ages 1-5 sleep **tucked in their own beds** about 10 to 12 hours each night. How many hours do you sleep at night?

3. During the day, a_____may **roost in a barn, tree, or cave**. Once asleep, this bird is not easily disturbed by loud daytime noises. It keeps its head upright while it sleeps.

4. An_____stands for about half of the four-to-six hours it sleeps each day. The other times it sleeps lying down. Most of its sleeping is in short little naps. When it is ready to lie down, it will sometimes **curl up its trunk and use it for a pillow**!

Answers: 1. common swifts, 2. human, 3. barn owl, 4. elephant

To the Creator, who gives us all the beautiful and fascinating animals in the world—SBS
To my wife, Laurie, for making art possible—GRP

Thanks to Susan Ring, Manager of Interpretation at the Roger Williams Park Zoo for verifying the accuracy of the information in this book.

Publisher's Cataloging-In-Publication Data

Slade, Suzanne.
Animals are sleeping / by Suzanne Slade ; illustrated by Gary R. Phillips.
p. : col. ill. ; cm.

Summary: The rhyming text provides information on the sleeping habits
of animals that live on land, in water, and fly through the air.
"For Creative Minds" section includes animals sorting cards and activities.
Interest age level: 002-006.
Interest grade level: P-1.
ISBN: 978-1-934359-10-5 (hardcover)
ISBN: 978-1-934359-26-6 (pbk.)

1. Sleep behavior in animals--Juvenile literature. 2. Animals--Sleep behavior.
3. Sleep. I. Phillips, Gary R. II. Title.
QL755.3 .S53 2008
591.5/19   2007935085

Printed in China

Sylvan Dell Publishing
976 Houston Northcutt Blvd., Suite 3
Mt. Pleasant, SC 29464